LOST TREASURES OF THE PIRATES OF THE CARIBBEAN

ALSO BY
JAMES A. OWEN

The Chronicles of the *Imaginarium Geographica*
Book One: *Here, There Be Dragons*

LOST TREASURES OF THE

JAMES A. OWEN & JEREMY OWEN

With Lon Saline & Mary McCray

SIMON & SCHUSTER BOOKS FOR YOUNG READERS
New York

Sydney

To Brett and Shawn, who believed in me back when I was just a little pirate,
sailed with me into unknown waters, following maps I made myself,
and know where all the real treasure lies.
—J. A. O.

To Churstan, for always being supportive;
and Alexander, for doing his best to interrupt the deadline
by arriving two weeks early.
—J. O.

ACKNOWLEDGMENTS

To Rubin Pfeffer, who had the idea, and supported us at every step;
David Gale, who suggested that we could do it within an impossible time frame (and knew we could);
Alexandra Cooper and Lizzy Bromley, for sharp edits and design;
and to Captain Charles Johnson, who is as real as we want him to be.

SIMON & SCHUSTER BOOKS FOR YOUNG READERS
An imprint of Simon & Schuster Children's Publishing Division
1230 Avenue of the Americas, New York, New York 10020
Text copyright © 2007 by James Owen
Illustrations copyright © 2007 by Jeremy Owen and James Owen
SIMON & SCHUSTER BOOKS FOR YOUNG READERS is a trademark of Simon & Schuster, Inc.
Book design by James A. Owen
The text for this book is set in Adobe Jenson Pro.
The illustrations for this book are rendered in pen and ink and digital media.
Manufactured in the United States of America
2 4 6 8 10 9 7 5 3 1
CIP data for this book is available from the Library of Congress.
ISBN-13: 978-1-4169-3960-3
ISBN-10: 1-4169-3960-1

Stories about pirates and their adventures have fascinated the world for many centuries. Over time fact and fiction have blended together. Tales of swashbuckling captains and the men who followed them, drawn by the promise of rich rewards, have ignited our imaginations. But not all of it is fiction. The pirates all had treasures that they hid away: in secret coves, on unknown islands, in abandoned ports. And to keep track of their hidden riches . . .

. . . they made MAPS. The treasure maps of the pirates were *real*. In the beginning pirates usually made the maps themselves so that no one else would know their secrets. But often these maps were of such poor quality, or so badly drawn, that the pirates couldn't find the way back to their own treasure!

That all changed in 1667, when the famed pirate Sir Henry Morgan decided that he needed maps that were both accurate and easy to read. So he sailed up the Atlantic coast to Charles Town (now called Charleston), South Carolina, where he enlisted the services of a retired silversmith named Elijah McGee. Thus began the greatest forgotten legend in pirate lore.

Elijah McGee excelled at making detailed maps and soon proved that he could be trusted to keep the pirate's secrets. Stories of Elijah's maps circulated, and in time he was found by other pirates, who also commissioned maps. And when Elijah grew too old to draw, his son, Eliot, simply stepped in and continued the trade; and after Eliot came his son, Ernest—and a dynasty was born.

In secret, three generations of McGees created treasure maps for the greatest pirates of the era. And while the maps themselves disappeared after the death of Ernest McGee, the legends about them continued to grow. A rumor spread in the 1880s that the McGees had even hidden clues in many of the maps they drew—clues that contained secret messages about the locations of pirates' treasure. Then in 1920, in Charleston, a merchant who counted both the McGees and the pirate François le Clerc among her ancestors found an old chest full of papers: letters of commission, bills of sale, harvest records—and maps.

No one has been able to tell if the maps really have clues to a lost treasure—but since the McGees' maps are real, then maybe the clues are too. And maybe, just maybe, there is still a treasure waiting for someone to find it. . . .

So—are you pirate enough?

The family McGee has been the subject of great curiosity among mapmakers for hundreds of years. Maps attributed to their craftsmanship can be found in many of the great libraries of the world.

The maps contained in this atlas were part of an estate sale held by Ernest's last descendant in 1995, and were sold to a private collector who was rumored to be a mapmaker himself.

It was not known at the time whether or not the McGee family ever kept for themselves more than the thirteen maps found by Ernest's descendant. However, recent examinations of other documents included with the so-called legacy maps suggest it was not only possible, but indeed, likely. . . .

MG

GREAT
SOUTH SEA

N

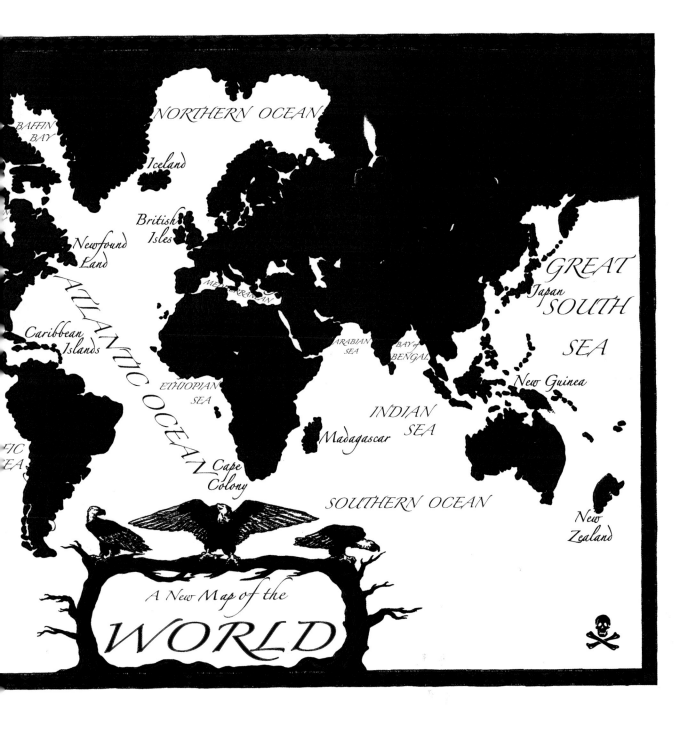

A New Map of the

WORLD

*I*n his book *A General History of the Robberies and Murders of the Most Notorious Pyrates,* Captain Charles Johnson called the pirate profession "The Great Mischief and Danger Which Threatens Kingdoms and Commonwealths."

That was in 1724, toward the end of the so-called golden age of pirates. But no record of a captain named Charles Johnson exists. Many people have speculated that the book was ghostwritten by a friend of Eliot McGee—Daniel Defoe. *A General History* exposed the piracy of the high seas in a way no one had done before, and all but created the modern conception of pirates.

The earliest pirates were called corsairs. Corsairs operated along the Barbary Coast and North Africa, to Greece and greater Europe beginning in the 1500s. They caused enough disruption that many countries negotiated treaties with them, essentially turning them into the second form of pirates: privateers, or government-licensed pirates.

But a third kind of pirate—the kind written about in *A General History*—flourished from the late 1600s to the early 1700s: the buccaneer. Originally a term for privateers who fought against the Spanish, "buccaneer" later became a blanket term for the pirate who found an ideal territory to plunder and pillage.

That territory was called the Caribbean.

BR

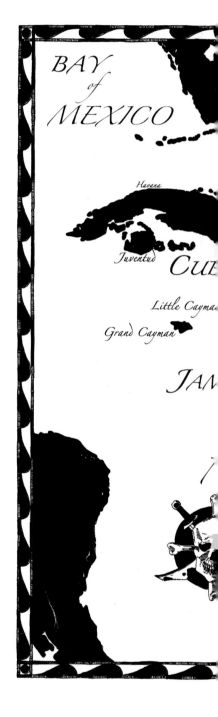

BAY *of* MEXICO

Havana

Juventud CU

Little Cayman

Grand Cayman

JA

WEST INDIES
and the
CARIBBEAN

Grand Bahama

Great Abaco

Elethera

Nassau

Andros

Cat Island

San Salvador

Great Exuma

Rum Cay

Long Island

Crooked Island

Acklins

Mayaguana

Great Inagua

Turks and Caicos Islands

n Brac

Tortuga

ATLANTIC OCEAN

Jeremie

St Thomas

Anguilla

St Martin

St John

St Barts

Negril

Ocho Rios

Puerto Rico

St Croix

Barbuda

CA

Port Royal

St Kitts

St Nevins

Antigua

HISPANIOLA

Montserrat

Guadeloupe

Dominica

Martinique

CARIBBEAN SEA

St Lucia

St Vincent

The Grenadas

Barbados

Aruba

Curacao

Bonaire

Grenada

Rouges

Orchita

Blanquilla

Tobago

Margarita

Tortuga

Trinidad

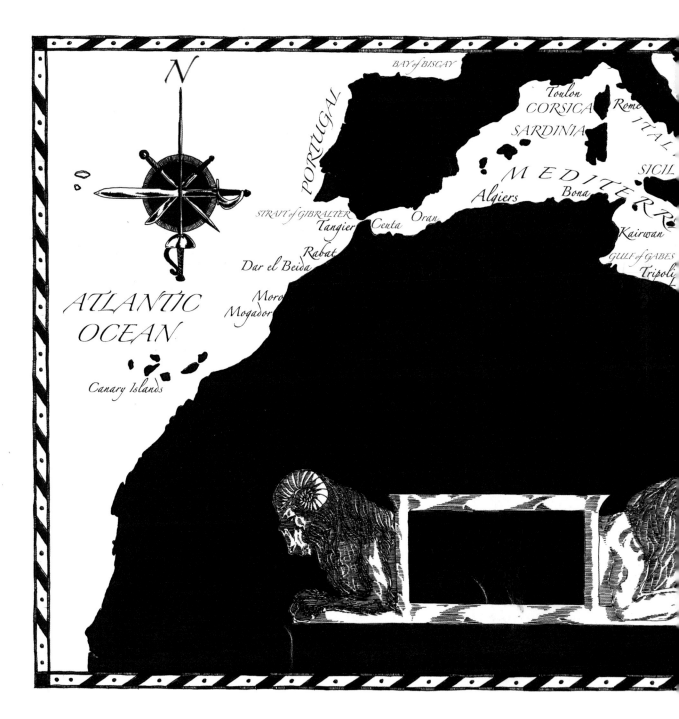

*P*iracy has existed for as long as there have been travelers on the seas of the world. The Greek and Roman cultures suffered under piracy for centuries before the advent of the great pirates of the Barbary Coast, in particular the infamous Barbarossa brothers. The African coastline offered great havens for pirates, especially in the port of Algiers, where the corsairs ringed the bowl-shaped coastline with battery forts that were nearly impossible to attack.

But as the Barbary pirates became more stabilized, so did the navies of the governments opposing them. The advantages of geography were no longer as favorable as they once were. So the pirates began to seek other territories—across the Atlantic. These buccaneers were the real-life pirates of the Caribbean.

UD

CAPTAIN JOHN RACKHAM

The Caribbean (then called the West Indies, or the Caribbee) offered three major advantages for piracy:

First, the number of small islands in the Caribbean is vast, providing many harbors where pirates could rest, repair their ships, and restock their stores without fear of being found. Thus, pirates like Captain John "Calico Jack" Rackham could maintain a home on Cuba, and then, as the need arose, go pillaging about the islands as he pleased.

Second, almost all of the commerce ships from Europe passed through the region on the way to America—an invitation to plunder.

And third, the man-of-war ships, used by the European navies, were simply too large to follow the pirate ships through the shallow lagoons and inlets. Thus the pirates could easily avoid capture.

It was the perfect place for piracy.

TW

BAY of N

N

W

S

Swan Islands

MEXICO

Andros

Cat Island

San Salvador

Great Exuma

Rum Cay

Long Island

Crooked Island

Ragged Islands

Acklins

Trinidad

CUBA

Cayman Brac

Grand Cayman

Little Cayman

CUBA

JAMAICA

Montego Bay

Ocho Rios

Jeremie

Negril

HISPANIOLA

Kingston

CARIBBEAN SEA

NORTH ATLANTIC OCEAN

W

TORTUGA

Cap Binauette

Voute L'Eglise

Point Saline

Terre Cassee

Point Macon

TORTUGA CANAL

Grande Point

Point Jean Rabel

Point Colette

Plaines

Point du Portugal

*T*he infamous golden age of piracy began in the late seventeenth century on Tortuga, a rather nondescript island to the north of Hispaniola (now Haiti and the Dominican Republic).

A melting pot of fugitive convicts and wayward laborers began hunting the herds of livestock that were abandoned on Tortuga when the Spanish settlers moved on. They were dirty and uncivilized, but strong, and their numbers grew. When the Spanish tried to drive out the newly named buccaneers by slaughtering all the livestock on the island, the plan backfired in a spectacular fashion.

The pirates organized themselves according to a strict code of conduct, elected captains, and began to claim passing ships. At first, the pirates' primary goal was to plunder foodstuffs, mainly meat. But ships often carried much more than food: Many carried silk, and slaves, and jewels—and gold.

The bounty was divided up on carefully prearranged terms, with extra portions going to the captain and ship's owner. Soon, this increasingly profitable enterprise spread to Hispaniola, and Jamaica, and Cuba—and then to America, where the privateers hired to defeat the pirates started turning to piracy themselves.

L K

CAPTAIN GEORGE LOWTHER

*T*he most successful of the buccaneers were not the Tortuga pirates, but rather the privateers who scourged the seas under commission to European and American rulers and leaders.

One privateer, Sir Henry Morgan (known as the Pirate Governor), was a man of high society who maintained his good standing with the British king even as he plundered Panama, Costa Rica, Cuba, and Jamaica. His own men accused him of keeping for himself the great fortunes they amassed, so Morgan hid his treasure. He then entrusted the location of his hidden bounty to one and only one man: the silversmith Elijah McGee.

EP

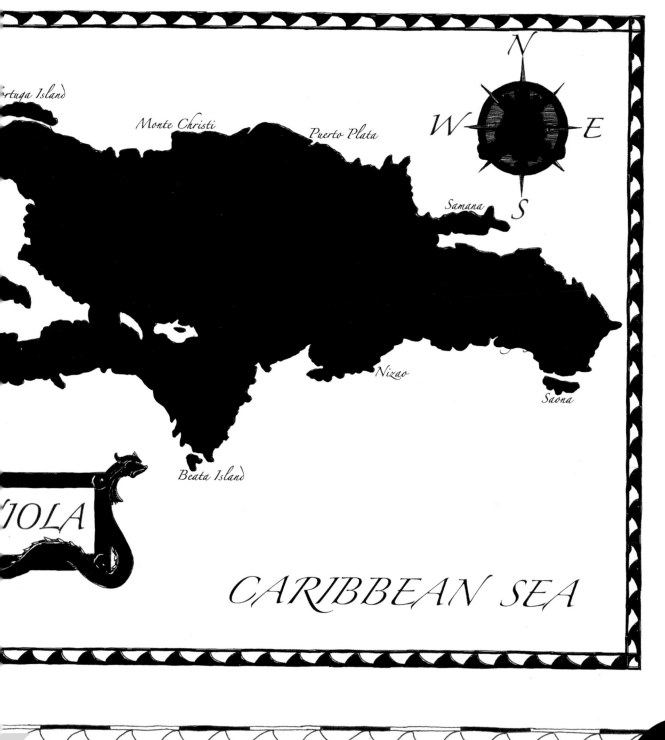

NASSAU
and the
ANTILLES

Little Abaco

Grand Bahama
Island

Great
Abaco
Island

North
Bimini

South
Bimini

N. W. PROVIDENCE CHANNEL

N. E. PROVIDENCE CHANNEL

Berry
Islands

Paradise
Island

Nassau

New Providence
Island

North
Eleuthera

Eleuthera
Island

NORTH ATLANTIC OCEAN

Andros
Island

Big Wood Cay

Yellow Cay

EXUMA SOUND

Water Cays

Cat Island

Great Exuma
Island

Conception
Island

San
Salvador

Rum Cay

N

Little Exuma

Long
Island

CROOKED ISLAND PASSAGE

Samana Cays

Crooked
Island

Long
Cay

Plana
Cays

Ragged
Islands

Acklins

MIRA POR VOS PASSAGE

Mayaguana
Island

Little Inagua

Great Inagua

*E*ljah's son, Eliot, having trained since his youth to take up his father's silversmithy, was instead brought into a secret brotherhood whose only other members were his father and the pirates themselves. Elijah McGee made maps mostly for Sir Henry Morgan, but as piracy boomed in the early eighteenth century, he became the mapmaker of choice for many other pirates.

Like Eliot himself, the pirates were young, many not yet twenty years old. And as buccaneering flourished, so did the prosperity of Eliot McGee. Eliot made maps for Captain Charles Vane, who was voted off his ship by his own crew for cowardice, and for Vane's successor, Captain John Rackham, as he terrorized the Bahamas and Hispaniola. He was also hired by the notorious female pirates Anne "Toothless Annie" Bonny and Mary Read, who murdered and pillaged their way through Nassau and the Antilles, and by Captain Edward England, whose banner was the well-known skull and crossbones. He made several maps for Captain George Lowther, who ranged the whole of the West Indies and conducted himself in such a gentlemanly manner that he seldom kept any treasure worth hiding.

And then came Captain Roberts.

IN

CAPTAIN BARTHOLOMEW ROBERTS

*I*n his own way Captain Bartholomew Roberts was as great a contributor to the legacy and mythology of the pirates as the legendary Blackbeard.

The romanticized image of the great dark-visaged pirate in a crimson waistcoat comes from Captain Roberts. His appearance was more gallant and dashing than fearsome—but he was, after all, still a pirate. If he was crossed, he took a terrible vengeance.

When the governors of Barbados and Martinique attempted to have him captured, he created a new flag bearing his own image standing on two skulls—each bearing one of the governors' initials. This replaced his original banner—the traditional black flag known to all as the Jolly Roger.

It was about this time that Eliot McGee began to seriously reconsider the means by which he earned his keep.

F V

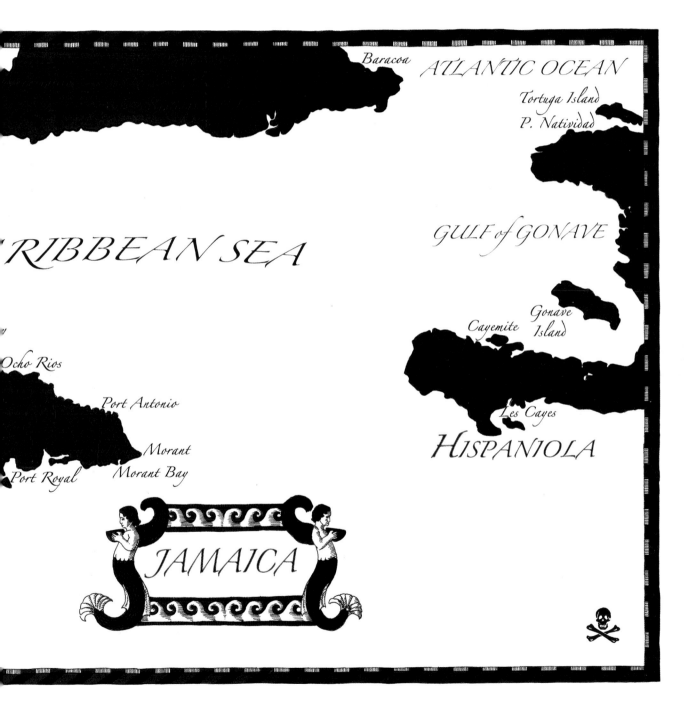

Baracoa

ATLANTIC OCEAN

Tortuga Island

P. Natividad

GULF of GONAVE

RIBBEAN SEA

Cayemite

Gonave Island

Ocho Rios

Port Antonio

Les Cayes

Morant

HISPANIOLA

Port Royal

Morant Bay

JAMAICA

Mosquito Point

INNER HARBOR

Rock Fort

Port Royal

Plum Point

CARIBBEAN SEA

PORT ROYAL

Gallows Point

Fort Carlisle

Kings House

Bridewell Prison
School
Courthouse

Fish and Fruit Markets

Smiths Alley

Common Sea Lane

Storehouses

St Pauls Church
Graveyard

Kings Wharf and Storehouses

Catt and Fiddle

Fort James

North Docks

Turtle and Meat Markets

Turtle Crawls

Morgans Line

Chocolata Hole

N

CARIBBEAN SEA

Fort

Fort Charles

THE

The French eventually took possession of Tortuga, and the pirates simply moved westward and established colonies on Jamaica.

Port Royal, at the southern end of Jamaica, was thought to be both the richest and wickedest city in the world, and was the center of pirate activity for many years. Sir Henry Morgan was based there, governed there, and even sat as a judge presiding over the trials of "true" pirates there.

Another Port Royal buccaneer, Captain Christopher Myngs, plundered cities on the South American coast—and the vast riches he seized flowed into his own pockets. His eventual arrest revealed the complicity of the city officials, which led to their downfall as well.

Like Morgan, Myngs entrusted the location of his riches to Elijah McGee but supposedly kept the maps somewhere in Port Royal. So when a devastating earthquake struck in 1692, plunging most of the city into the sea, it was believed that many of the pirates' maps were also lost.

SQ

CAPTAIN CHARLES VANE

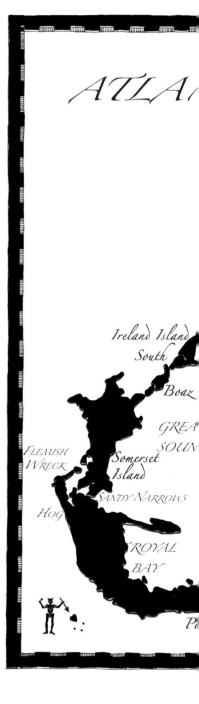

*T*he greatest pirate, the one who inspired the most nightmares and influenced every fictional pirate from Captain Hook to Long John Silver, was indisputably Edward Teach—better known as Blackbeard.

He carried three pairs of flintlocks on flamboyant sashes, as well as several daggers and cutlasses. He braided his namesake beard with colorful ribbons and wove gunpowder into them—which he would light to create a terrifying, unearthly halo around his head.

Blackbeard was not averse to killing one of his own men every so often, just to maintain his fearful reputation. During one of those savage moods he fired a pistol under a table, hitting a crewman in the kneecap and forever crippling him. That man never forgot, nor did he forgive.

CY

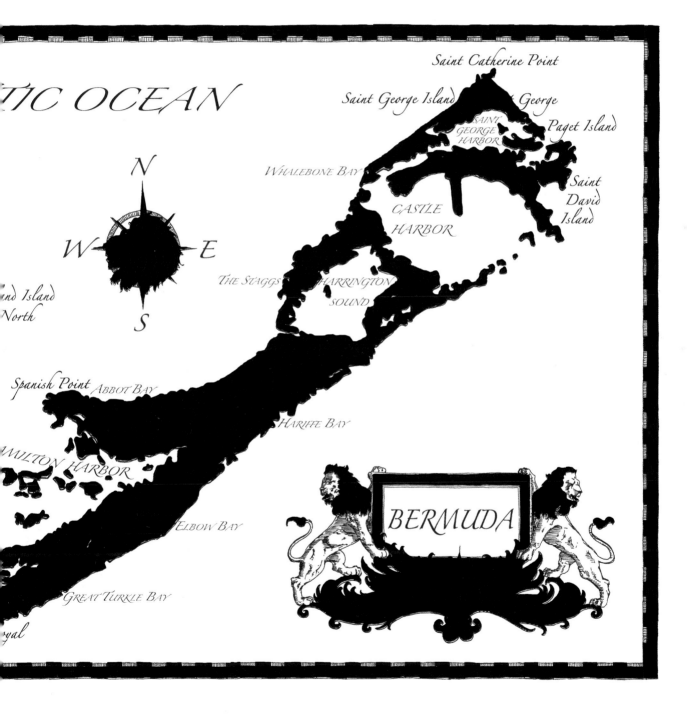

ATLANTIC OCEAN

BARBADOS

North
Point

Speightstown

Parish of
St. Joseph

Parish of
St. J

Hole Town

Conset
Point

Ragged
Point

Kitridge
Point

Parish of
St. Philip

Foul
Bay

Bridge Town
Carlisle
Bay

Green
Point

Long Bay

Oistins
Bay

South
Point

N

TO THE
LESSER
ANTILLES

*W*hen at long last Blackbeard was defeated and his crew put to trial, only two of his men escaped being killed in the fierce, final battle or by the gallows that awaited the survivors. One was the man crippled by Blackbeard—Israel Hands.

Hands had been master of Blackbeard's sloop, and its captain before that. He was granted a pardon by the British Crown and allowed to return to London, where he met a man who would help him get revenge against his former captain.

The man Israel Hands met was Daniel Defoe, who at that time was writing the novel *Robinson Crusoe*. Defoe was no stranger to the activities of pirates, but Hands told him a secret few others knew: He told Defoe about Elijah and Eliot McGee. In short order, Eliot McGee and Defoe became great friends. Together, they invented Charles Johnson—the great pirate biographer who didn't exist. The McGee family had compiled much information about the pirates during the decades they served as the mapmakers to the buccaneers; and Defoe was an accomplished novelist. Thus was born the great definitive account of the pirates: *A General History of the Robberies and Murders of the Most Notorious Pyrates*.

A O

CAPTAIN KIDD

*E*liot and Defoe published *A General History* under the name Charles Johnson in 1724, but their most ambitious project was never fully realized.

They had planned to publish a book they referred to as "the Pyratlas": a compilation of the many maps the McGee family had created. They would then make their fortune by selling the buccaneers' own maps to the national navies that were being built up by governments around the world.

However, their project was derailed by Defoe's death in 1731, and by the time Eliot's son, Ernest, managed to assemble the book in 1759, most of the worst pirates—such as Blackbeard, who had been beheaded—were dead, while the rest had become privateers, sanctioned by the very nations who had fought them years earlier. The age of the buccaneer was over, and with it, interest in the buccaneer map.

XH

CARIBBEAN SEA

San Blas Point
San Blas Islands

GULF of
MUITOS

Los Perlas
Islands

GULF of
S. MICHEL

N

BAY

of

PANAMA

de Paereu   Point Mala

UTH SEA

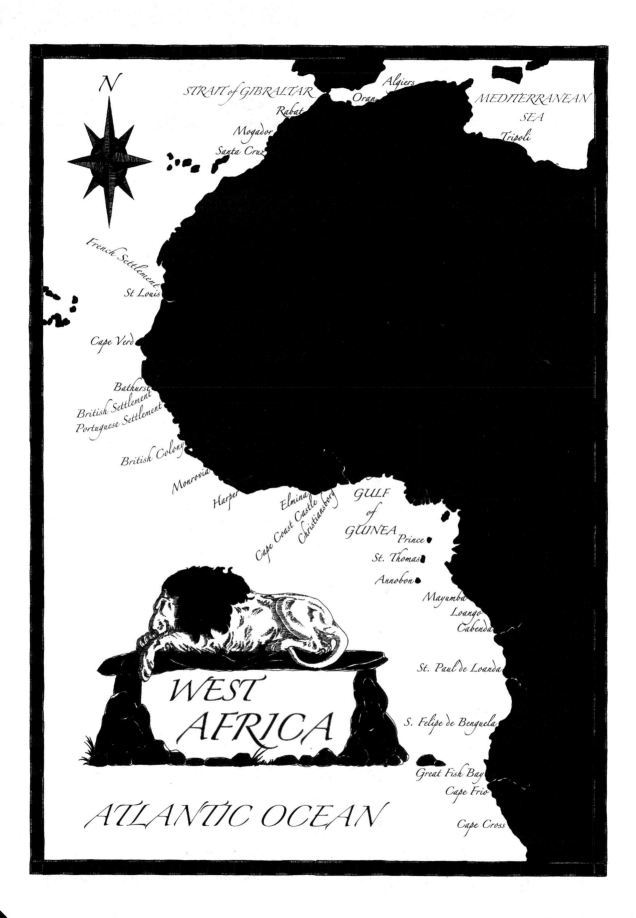

N

STRAIT of GIBRALTAR

Algiers

Oran

Rabat

MEDITERRANEAN
SEA

Mogador

Tripoli

Santa Cruz

French Settlement

St Louis

Cape Verd

Bathurst
British Settlement
Portuguese Settlement

British Colony

Monrovia

Harper

GULF
of
GUINEA

Elmina
Cape Coast Castle
Christiansborg

Prince

St. Thomas

Annobon

Mayumba
Loango
Cabenda

St. Paul de Loanda

WEST
AFRICA

S. Felipe de Benguela

Great Fish Bay
Cape Frio

ATLANTIC OCEAN

Cape Cross

*F*or a brief time, pirates who knew of the McGee legacy continued to request Eliot's services until his death in 1746 in Algiers, the newly revived, post-golden-age capital of piracy.

Rather than work for the current pirates, Ernest used the records from the unfinished Pyratlas to make maps related to pirates long dead. He began with the Barbarossa brothers, who were legendary along the Barbary Coast; the great corsair François le Clerc, the scourge of Cuba who was known as Peg Leg in the Lesser Antilles; and the notorious Captain Kidd, whose escapades ranged from the Leeward Islands all the way to Madagascar.

None of Ernest's friends could figure out why he was engaged in his work, until they realized he was not simply *making* maps to pirate treasures—he was *finding* the treasures themselves. He spent much time abroad, but it was while he was in London in late 1768 that a fire broke out, destroying three generations of work.

Accounts of the fire told how McGee managed to salvage specific maps—presumably ones that led to actual treasures—and fled into the night. No sign of treasure was found in the ruins.

On his deathbed two years later, Ernest would only say that he had hidden the maps somewhere in the Caribbean, with the pronouncement that "they were created for pirates—let pirates find them."

JZ

Included with the maps that were discovered at the estate sale (which had been intended for the original Pyratlas nearly 250 years ago) was a riddle created by Eliot McGee, Ernest McGee, and Daniel Defoe. In the spring of 2006 the compilers of this book took possession of the legacy maps of the McGees and with them, the responsibility for the greatest secret of all: There is a fourteenth map. A secret map. The last map made by Ernest McGee.

Only those who solve the riddle will be allowed to see the map. The keys to solving the riddle are within the pages of this book. Every story, and every map, and every page contains a clue—but the riddle itself is a pirate song:

> *Though death may have claimed us, our treasure be hid.*
> *The last of their duties our mapmakers' bid,*
> *To secret away from the bright eyes a-prying,*
> *From scoundrels a-seeking and fear'd foes trying*
> *To claim as their own the treasure unshared,*
> *With cannon a-blazing and scimitar bared.*
> *Following footsteps from ages gone past,*
> *A pirate at heart may find it at last:*
> *First, to the city that fell in the sea; and second, the home of Calico Jack;*
> *Third, Turtle Island is where you must be; fourth, east, to Algiers, before turning back;*
> *Fifth finds both Port Royal and Great Turkle Bay; and by Bonny and Read the next lands were plundered;*
> *Last comes a fair mermaid who's pointing the way; seek quickly now, pirates—before what's hidd'n be sundered.*

Drawn on the back of each original map was a key that represented one of two letters. Those keys and their corresponding letters have been reproduced across from the maps in this atlas. The riddle holds the clues to the maps that will lead to the seven-letter answer that unlocks the secret fourteenth map.

Follow in the footsteps of Ernest McGee. Discover the secrets of the pirates. And maybe you'll be the one to discover the lost treasures of the pirates of the Caribbean.

So—are you pirate enough?

To enter your answer to the riddle, claim your prize if you're correct, and
download more pirate lore, go to www.simonandschuster.com/losttreasures.